THE CONFESSIONS OF A MORTAL REBEL

Devansh Arora

TANEESHA PUBLISHERS

Title : The Confessions of a Mortal Rebel
Author : Devansh Arora
Edition : First (June, 2025)
ISBN : 9789349789395

Published by

TANEESHA PUBLISHERS | *A Venture by -* **PRACHI DIGITAL PUBLICATION**

Regd. Add.: 254, Khuriyakhatta No. 10, Bindukhatta,
Lalkuan, Nainital - 262402, Uttarakhand, India
Website : www.taneeshapublishers.in
E-mail : taneeshapublishers@gmail.com
Phone : +91 8454 812712, +91 8057 812712

Printed by :
Manipal Technologies Limited, Bengaluru - 560001, Karnataka

Table of Contents

The Unveiling Ritual

Naked
Similar to a coven engulfing flames in a glade
Dancing freely to the percussion of a drum
Unafraid by the stories of ambushes in the woods
He discovered cryptic animals with horns of the Devil
An obsession with the perilous ceremony
And he was no longer ashamed of exhibiting his art

The Descent

Chosen for Earth, like Jews for the concentration camps,
A parentally powered psycho cast us down with blindfolds.
Yet, I embraced the depth,
While others terrified themselves with the certainty of the fall.
No one paused to hear the rustling leaves, whispering philosophies to those who seek wisdom.
The race for survival and speed
Drowned the intelligence of the self-absorbed.

In the end, a river of blood awaited
The meteors descending from the sky —
owed the debt of consuming heaven's forbidden minerals,
To the invincible spirit of Adolf Hitler.

Flesh Residue

Hoist up like a flag
Flow down like sap
Inhale breath through the filter of death
Count in reverse as circumstances turn adverse
You may walk or rush
Shout out loud or hush
Be the best to become the worst
Humans are nothing but cigarettes
Gradually converting into ashes to be flushed

Corporate Interview

Across the wooden ocean,
Dwells a suited man —
Bound by a narrow necktie of perception,
Yet unbounded in his swelling gut.
He wields a fishing rod,
Luring the gullible to feed his insatiable hunger.
My colleagues hail him as a superhero;
But I reserve my shovel — To dig his grave,
Should he reveal himself
As nothing more than a villain in an adult film.

The End of the World

I witnessed a glimpse of Apocalypse
As if a war through the vision of a soldier
Wind flew across me like knives and bullets
And the pawed shrieked for help
I wanted to help them but refrained
Succumbing to the handcuffs of calamitous callousness

Christ

A colourless ball slid down from the pinnacle
Blotted different complexions on the pathway
Ghastly alleys impatiently awaited the colours to resuscitate
Blues rained from Heaven to wreak havoc, crippling the messiah to recreate

Sugar Daddy

She is an alien to my intellect
Squints me as if I linger in the dump
Considers my feet belong to the edge
And the possibility to slump
Repulsive to shake my hand
Ladies & gentlemen, do I appear numb?
We know you are a dignified woman
Courteously snuggling the abuse of your man,
bowing down to the grace of his sum

Possessed

I stepped inside my bathroom, leaving the door ajar,
Inviting a shadow to crawl across the floor.
Startled by the hiccups of a coughing faucet,
I wrestled with the grumbling regulator.
Then I saw her —
Slithering through the narrow tunnel to possess me.
She inhaled the last fumes of my decency,
Igniting a cult within my corrupted soul.
Blame her for my madness.
Imprison her for the repugnance. But spare me.

Pens, Chalk & Broken Rules

Your head can sharpen crayons but I have a pen
Please allow me to shove its tip into your condescending lens
And as you break your own rule creating nuisance
I shall signal my colleagues to séance and dance
Conquer the pedantic scribblings of the board
Pounce on the teacher and steal his chalk
You have confiscated the hunter from his sword
Let your veiled allies shift upon the benches,
While we tear through their false disguises.
Embrace the performers upon their wooden stages,
And ascend as better masters without academic degrees.

Demonic Discrimination

I was a destined loser at the party. Others won the game with paternal wealth. Intensive lights shone and blinded my vision from viewing unreachable luxury whereas drums hammered my ears away from the discussion of purchasing an expensive car. I ran positions with my notepad for the owners of books. I stood outside a car in freezing winters and missed the whiskey of summers.

Miss Cocaine

Pensively carrying a doubt,
You bit the pen in your mouth
The professor helped others as you waited in a line
I wanted to snort you and filter others out
He seemed like the host of a famous restaurant, reserving tables for the incoming guests
I wondered why a queen like you did not skip the queue or his tests
It must have something to do with mundane morals which I never understand
You also held a hefty book in your hand, seeking answers for questions irrelevant to the story of you and I
Pissed, I wanted to snatch away your instruments of education
And set you free

Apricity

Abandon your companions
You are confined inside the worldly perimeters
Leap the boundaries of solipsism, falsehood and greed
There is a garden across the corridors of slaves
Choose the generous one my child
Rustle through the grasses and bless a bench
Can you sense the power of sunlight in winters?
Seize the peace and pacify your soul
Grab my hand to the friendless pole
Befriend her, she is harmless
Swing, sweeping your dress through the concrete
Resuscitate the lifeless game for you can

Knees that Touched

She hitchhiked the autorickshaw I rode on
Hopped in and settled down beside
A subtle connection with her knee was suffice to
demoralize the wise
And now, if the chances of a natural conversation do not
arise
Remorse would hoist upon quitting this ride
And I might blame myself again for cowardice

From Blindness to You

I quit the fog and became discernible
Exposed to sophisticated menaces
Anxiety cuffed my hands
And then I sensed some difference in the atmosphere
My nose sniffed a prodigious medication
The predicament restored my vision
And you became the first woman I came across
A doctor in disguise

Firefighter

Engulfed by suffocating buildings,
In the garden where cows were tormented to death by professional butchers
I connected with a compassionate uniform
She criticized the neglected massacre, while firmly holding her water bottle
Intrigued by the grip, I questioned my intellect
Did the grasp insinuate an exceptional empathy for the exanimate molecules or the fear of losing a courteous companion?
She requested my partnership to the corridor regularly blessed by her footsteps
A couple of shadows copied our laughter while following us
And then she slung a laden bag on her shoulder
I longed to relieve her burden but lacked the bond
I escorted her to a blazing bus in the parking lot
Why did she bid adieu to her fire extinguisher?

The Divine Encounter

She traveled the deprived road alone for years.
I read her travelogue inscribed on a magnificent leaf.
Spellbound by the depth of her words and the grace of her handwriting, I followed the trail of her footsteps.
She resided beneath a tree-shed near the pond,
Gifted by the Almighty with imaginations to pass her days.

I struck the door to heaven — no one answered.
So I waited for her, speaking to the fishes that glided within the pond.

At last, as evening fell, I was granted her sight.
Street lamps, hanging beneath the branches, were ignited by lingering ghosts to erase the overwhelming darkness.
The lamps swayed and danced with the twilight winds.
She held my hand beneath the light of hope, and blessed me.

Only then did I realize — she was not human, but a goddess. The one who chose me.
And I shall forever remain grateful for her blessings.

Permanent Across Pixels

Your accommodation shifts to my phone with distance.
A hallucination of your body appears across the screen.
Your tummy rests upon the keyboard,
And I tickle you with my fingers as I type messages for your amusement.
Even when I minimize the app with a simple swipe,
You refuse to fade away —
A quiet sign of permanency

Pen Wrapped in your Hair

These hair battle the sun to cool your head.
I beg you to release them from the restricting grip of your band,
For they long to caress your soft cheeks.

And when you ride your scooty with me as your pillion,
Let the wind carry your hair onto my face.
I'll close my eyes and breathe in their scent —
The scent of your memories, both good and bad, like seeds rooted in your scalp.

I will inhale them, cleansing your head once again.
Then I'll write about you with a pen tangled in your strands
—
Whatever you wish to hear,
Whatever you desire to listen.

Tandava

I wandered to an alley,
Alone,
Puffing away my blues.

I paused before a camera with an attached flashlight,
Surveilling nightmares.
I stared deep into the spotless glitter—
And disappeared.

I wiped my vision with intrigue.
Across the flames, stood a woman,
Dancing wildly with her feet on the sun.

My steps crossed the line instinctively.
I was surprised that my existence refused to vanish into smoke.
Instead, I felt a warmth like never before.

Gradually, the entire scene morphed into the palm of her hands.
I was home.

When her Tears Fell

Teardrops on her cheeks,
Slithering down like rocks tumbling from a mountain.
I cannot bear their weight.

She deserves the warmest sunlight and perfect composure.
Even a minor crack in her mental stability wounds me.

She stands strong and firm, guiding travelers,
Helping them reach their destinations.

It is her deep, unwavering empathy
That makes me love her.

Saved by Her

I quit my usual position and climbed the rope to the top for a while.
She stood near the fence, gazing at the mountains.
I was surprised by my failure to admire nature —
For my vision was blocked by the composure of her existence.
Do you know who controls the wind?
I want to thank that force for granting divinity to the goddess,
Tossing her hair like whispered silk.
Spellbound, I lost my balance and nearly slipped back to the bottom.
But she caught my hand and pulled me up,
Granting me the priceless privilege of standing upon the special platform with her.

Fetish

I despise your pants
Scissor them please, and tease
Help me decode the patterns on your knees
I want to study your legs
Become a sexual dope
Caress your ham as passionately as a soap
Embellish into your only hope to acquire those
Heavenly sensations

Pedestrian

Innumerable vehicles cruised down the highway
Nobody let her cross the road
She considered I was one of them
But my scooter braked to a halt
I proved her wrong -
The woman was surprised
But she ignored my courtesy and I died

Ditched

When cash became as useless as the butt of cigarettes
I pulverised the motive to endeavor beneath my shoe
An opaque structure repulsed me from humanly relevance
And then the walls began to close in
Hypocritically frightened by the sight of a quick death
I smote the hindrance
Only to realize I was banished by her
And now my death was certain

Blackout

I escaped the structure while heaving a rifle
Bullets shone awaiting my presence in the garden
Holed cans of beer whirled in confrontation
A reminder about the prostitutes I knocked in the night
My vision stumbled upon the ashtray on the table
Where is the blemish of their lipstick on the butt of cigarettes?
And then the couch
Why are the letters on their T-shirts censored?
I solemnly questioned my conscience again
Who sipped on my humor?
Speak up
I hate the sight of muffled wild dogs

The Godless Man

He quit the mural of solitude and barged through the crowd
He hid his monstrosity by putting on a shroud
A psychopath strolled the footpaths of your town
He was guided to a cemetery by a thunderous cloud
The innocent men he murdered were all down
He mercilessly stabbed them to steal their money
And now he wished to baptify himself with an apology
But they refused to acknowledge his request
Disappointed, he continued with his quest
And then a signboard questioned him before the bright dead end
Should he turn right or left?

The Other Side

There is an invisible wall
Opaque for bustling lives
Glassy for the deprived
Spectators judge
When players indulge
How would the impaired erase this smudge?

The Hypocrite's Gaze

Little dresses brew golden wines;
You sip the glass intimately with your spouse.
Yet when your eyes wander to their exhibition in the market,
You scan the shelves with a seedy gaze,
As saliva stains your lips, revealing your intentions.
Why observe what you label vile, if your heart claims to be pure?
A creation of your Father, condemned as profane —
Hypocrisy draped in traditions and decency.

Her Moment

She arrived at the institute ahead of time, while the corridors still breathed calm — As if it were morning on her farm.
My baby strode through the aisles of tables and chairs,
Her footsteps echoing in the stillness.
She never truly grasped the magnitude of her presence in this classroom of competition.
In that moment, I watched her transform —
From a sidekick to the protagonist of her story.
For the first time, she owned the entire room, choosing her seat with authority.
I felt content,
Watching her embrace this freedom she had earned.

Cure

I wiped the mist from my glass
And envisioned you oxygenate the water inside by swimming the mass
I dropped you some icy crystals for assistance
And then gulped you into my bloodstream
Which led to the extension of my existence

Sanctuary

Across the wilderness of surrendering to my family's expectations,
I discovered the glade where I could finally be myself.
I confined my existence within the shelter of her perception,
While others pierced me with manipulative gazes.
Bearers of jealousy struck my stomach with rifle butts,
Yet failed to breach the boundaries of shatterproof trust.
Together, we embraced fantasies,
Abandoning the rigid practicalities of science.
And beneath the radiant light of positivity,
Blessed by the sunshine,
I stumbled upon my soulmate.

Electric Love

Little comets dangle from your fists at night,
As you glide across the bumpy pavements of your hilltop town.
The bright streetlights surrender their purpose when you appear,
And even the lake loses its charm before your glow.
Yet I gather the courage to dive — For I know,
There is someone on the ground
Who will save my life.

The Guiding Angel

My feet trembled before the great divide,
Tears abandoned my eyes in disoriented confusion. I was destined to choose the path of freedom,
Yet the weight of respectable acquaintances
And the voices of ancestors
Pierced me with the dagger of conservatism.
Then —
An angel from the promised land steered her cloud towards me.
She descended upon one of the countless platforms that adorned her grace,
And with a healing spell,
She drew the dagger from my chest.
With tenderness, she gifted me her wisdom,
And gently pulled my hand
Towards the righteous path.

Suicide

I curtain the windows,
Blocking sunrays from bleeding through.
I pluck out my eyes,
And surrender my tears to silence.
An exhausted soul whispers my heartbeat to stillness,
Upon the deathbed I carved —
To finally rest in peace.

Cutlery and Consequences

Quit chasing crumbs to feed your dread,
No feast will suit your shifting mood.
Down the lane, a café waits.
You need no key, no word, no plea—
The doors will slide with soulless grace.
From cracks in stone, a couple crawls,
To shove you towards your chosen place.
You cannot flee. You must obey. Pick a booth and face the
hush. The waiter comes with hollow eyes,
A grin carved deep to make you blush.
"Shall I pour you blood or wine?" He asks without a voice
or breath. Here, all orders lead to one thing— A quiet,
slow, exquisite death.

Peer Pressure

These wishes are the rusted nails inside my skull,
Driven deep by the hands I once admired.
The hammers pounded by my peers and idols with each blow sang a lullaby I mistook for belonging.
They told me: "Be proud, be good, be one of us."
So, I swallowed the rules, the rituals, the roles.
I danced on strings and wore their masks —
Until the echo of my name faded into obedience.
But then I felt a rot beneath the applause, the ache of bones that bent too long.
And in that hidden, hollow chamber, I decided - I would not belong.
I mapped my escape in silence and scars, uncoiling the wires wrapped around my spine. But the truth, I found, was a lonely god,
And freedom asked for more than just defiance.
So here I sit now, unscrewed but split,
Neither prisoner nor prophet, just incomplete.
And maybe the curse was never the hammer —
But my own perception.

Racehorse

A racehorse bred with a compulsion
To gallop, to gleam, to grind past the finish line. Not for freedom, not for pride—
But for the bets placed in ink and greed,
By patrons clutching paper like prophecy.
Its hooves strike the ground like contracts signed,
Each stride a repayment of silent debts.
Muscles ripple with imposed purpose,
Driven not by desire, but dividends.
This creature—sleek, admired, paraded— Carries more than flesh and sinew.
It bears the burden of investments,
Of expectations too sharp to shed.
And yet, it smiles in interviews. It poses. It performs.
Clothed in the camouflage of competition, it whispers to itself,
"I am an athlete. I am free."
But beneath the varnish of televised valor, Lurks the truth:
A contemporary slave — Branded not with chains, but with applause.

Rubicon

Breathing in excruciation —
As if death coexists with life.
Psychic murderers, daggers in hand,
Point toward a path cloaked in fog,
Compelling the surrender
Of a despised, dwindling will.
And so I step — Into the Rubicon,
Where choice is illusion
And return, forbidden.

A Brief Transaction

It was supposed to be business. A brief rendezvous.
Nothing more.
But goddamn —
She stepped out of the shadows like regret in heels,
And became art in motion.
Something sacred crawling through filth.
Time didn't stop. It held its breath.
I gave her the package,
But she took more than that — A few words,
And the last untouched corner of my mind.
She said she lived in a PG. I imagined the walls.
The curfews.
The warden.
I'd murder that warden, slow. Not out of rage —
But devotion.
To reach her room.
Not for lust — But to talk.
To share something unpermitted.
To let her breathe the air without regulation.
We'd speak of chains,
Of systems,
Of blood as currency.
And if she asked who did it, I'd show her my hands - Still warm.
And say:
This is the price of wanting you free.

The Performer

He walks a tightrope
Strung across a sea of fire — Each step a negotiation
With pain dressed as purpose.
He calculates his heartbeats like debts —
Precise, predictable,
Performing balance for no one's applause.
An angel hovers near,
Not divine, not cruel — just present. She confuses his rhythm,
But corrects his tilt,
Keeps him alive enough to suffer another act.
But he is no fool —
Just a clown worn to bone, paint peeling, smile cracked.
Long before the edge arrives, he makes his choice.
He steps off.
Not because he couldn't — But because he wouldn't.
Let the rope burn,
Let the waters boil.
He quits the stage
Before it consumes him whole.

Serpents of Obedience

Leashes crawl towards me like serpents,
Hissing promises of peace
As they prepare to strangle.
To press me into a grave
The obedient call home.
I fight to escape. But their words —
Their perfect little knives — Cut deeper than the chains.
I need an angel.
Not the kind from scripture,
But one who'll dive into the filth, clutch my shaking hand,
And kiss it like a vow — That I'm still worth saving.

Where the Beasts Don't Bite

Undervalue me.
Aim better.
Throw your snowballs at this exposed flesh. They bruise colder than fists.
Near the slope,
I buried a passage —
A quiet escape from this toxic mountain of closeness,
Where love feels like suffocation wearing a friendly face.
Below, a freezing forest waits - Beyond the glow of bright lights
And forced affection.
Don't worry, I've got a plan.
To dodge the teeth of death,
I'll offer cigarettes to the beasts.
Maybe they'll cough
Instead of bite.
Maybe they'll laugh.
Maybe I will too.

Burning Alone

A strange, unheeded cigarette
Ashening
Without kisses
Is magical
Repulsive
Quittable
Bestowing life
Not cancer

The Painter

She filed her tools
To summon the storm of creation.
Fixed the canvas on its trembling frame,
And drew a pair of angels
In flight,
Or maybe in fall.
Then —
Without warning,
Her shadow slipped from the tedious floor,
And spilled itself
Across the barren white.
Darkness engulfed the lovers,
Not to erase —
But to test their glow.
Applaud the painter
Who dared to drench them in shadow,
Then dressed their broken outlines in color.
So they could shimmer again.

Not Just Another Day

Morning arrived — My alarm rang,
Singing its familiar, forced melody. I rose,
Abandoning the warmth of dreams,
And shuffled to the bathroom, Half-asleep,
Half-someone else.
My stare met the mirror — Frowning, distracted, lost
In the plans I'd made for the day.
I brushed my teeth, preparing my lips
To greet hers.
I bathed away the bitterness of prolonged seclusion,
And dressed myself
In something I hoped she'd admire.
Then laced my shoes — Not just to walk,
But to arrive.
At the café she chose. With the smile I chose. For her.

Crimson Ritual

I am the vampire —
A creature of midnight thirst, seeking asylum
In the tangled dusk of your hair.
You, the witch —
Wielding vision like a spell, binding me
With every blink.
You tempt me
To pause at your neck— To hover, not devour — To let desire
Outweigh instinct.
Your lips —
Stained in ceremonial red, call to me.
A blaze bottled in wax and pigment,
More potent than blood itself.
And I,
The willing predator, feed not on flesh,
But on the ruin you wear so beautifully.

The Border

She is a goddess, harboring a promised land
Within her bioluminescent glow.
He longed
To cross that sacred border,
To bathe in the light
She didn't know she radiated.
But there were guards— Both seen and unseen,
Clad in doubt, fear,
And fragments of her past.
They did not speak.
They simply detained him— At the edge
Of something divine.

The Ramp and the Radiance

A glimmering embodiment of vogue,
She moved with effortless grace — Spellbinding even the myopic,
Bending blurred vision into awe.
With a flick of her wand on the ramp of life.
She ignited a blaze of glory — Unscripted,
Unapologetic.
And I —
A bystander lost in the crowd — Was blessed
To witness a single frame of her unfolding legend.

Cartography of Her

She wore an abyss,
And I fell —
Not by accident, but with reverence.
I charted her like sacred terrain —
Traced the stillness of her flora,
And endured the shrieks of her restless fauna.
But I spent too long
Searching for a fall of water
That never welcomed me.
The rock shelter —
Her refuge, her secret — Was already carved
By men with hollow hands.
And I,
The only fool
Who loved the whole forest.

Her Halo was Hollow

He found her — A burning angel
Smoking by the roadside of July,
Wings charred
Like promises in a preacher's ashtray.
She looked holy.
But hell hid behind her eyeliner
And half-spoken names.
He didn't read the signs — Didn't see the serpent coiled in her halo.
She baptized him
In sweat, pills,
And holy apathy.
Turned his Psalms into ransom notes,
His wine into sedatives,
And his prayers into late-night tweets no one answered.
She didn't kill him.
She just rewrote his gospel — Verse by verse —
Until God stopped listening.

Canvas Desecration

She is a shamaness,
Lips lit like forbidden candles
Which guide his ruinous gaze.
He rots in a crooked shelter,
A few aching miles from her door,
Sketching her name in dust
On cracked windowpanes.
He prays for wings,
Not to escape,
But to rise — Just high enough
To glimpse her linen rituals
Framed by the glass of a second-story heaven.
But longing is not relief. Peace only arrives
When he shatters the painter's wrist, crushes the pigment,
And desecrates the image
That dares hold her beauty without his consent.

666

There's a hotel on the hill
Wearing a sky-colored umbrella — Perpetually raining
Even when the clouds are dry.
I stepped in alone.
The lights flickered like a heartbeat on drugs. Then the elevator opened —
And there she was.
Hair black as basement water,
Skin the shade of forgotten statues. A quiet echo of Bloody Mary,
Tamed into elegance.
She didn't speak.
Just pressed the sixth button — Three times.
The elevator shuddered
And began its descent.
But I never saw the doors open. I woke up
Clutching a pillow like it had answers.

Entitled Pilgrim

I deserve that place
More than its owner ever could. There
She gifted me her blues — Not to burden,
But to cradle.
Maps and landmarks? They're for strangers.
I could find the monument blindfolded.
All it takes is the memory of her freshly trimmed hair,
Dancing in the wind,
And the echo
Of her flexing me
Like a trophy of tenderness.
Once,
My thoughts held weight. Now, they float —
But I remain flattered by how briefly
I mattered.

Resignation Letter

My limbs froze from obsession. I couldn't move,
Couldn't lift another box.
Employers fold the bold. And scold the sold.
I belonged to the second category.
She was the root,
The center of my unrest.
So I swung an axe,
Tearing the possession from its pedestal.
She collapsed — Lifeless.
But as her head hit the floor,
Flowers sprouted from her neck,
Unapologetically blooming.
I lit a cigarette,
Sat beside her still body, And held it like closure.
That moment—
Smoky, final, quiet — Confirmed
My resignation.

Threshold Between Realms

I squinted at the stars,
Searching for a misstep —
A slip into the stream of imagination.
I longed to taste the Other Realm before the log widened,
Before the crossing became impossible.
The nightlight cuffed my wrists —
Forcing me to endure what loomed ahead.
But daylight returned like a sovereign,
Granting me the power to rewrite my storyline.

Highway to Her

He dove into the perilous depths of a highway —
Swimming against steel tides, straining for the shore.
She squinted at her wristwatch,
Each tick echoing the palpitation of hope and fear —
Awaiting his return.
He dodged the razor-blades of sharks
Just to breathe in the forgotten scent of her skin.
Memories of their fevered nights flashed like headlights
— Blinding, dazzling.
A contumacious tide— Jealous of the radiance— Surged
from the dark
And squealed him down into death.

Holy Combustion

Deprived of sexism, blown by both —
Men and women.
A cigarette is the epitome of equalitarian grace.
Mother of smoke, sacred,
She births what is subtle, free and untouchable.
Like God —
Appearing in a heartbeat,
Blessing the lungs,
And then vanishing
As if never existed.

Moksha

Eyes ablaze
Vessels rupturing beneath the heat
Nightmares slither
Flickering like a broken film
Funeral pyres exhale their shrieks into hollow skies
Flares tearing at the fabric of emptiness
The spirit fractures its mortal bindings,
Piercing through the veils of forbidden realms.
It drifts —
Naked.
Unclaimed.
Devoured by the cold hunger of the void.

The Wrath shall Pass

When the boats become clouds,
And I drown into the vigorous purple,
Do not rescue me with the ropes of thunder. Instead, honor the storm of destruction.
For I wish your God to succeed in his cherished endeavor — To punish the sinners
Who dared to indulge in worldly attachments: Friends, family, and others.